Caterpillar dreams

Discussing the story is a good way to spend time together and will encourage your child to use her imagination. Talk about why Hugo would want to be a lion instead of a caterpillar. What are your child's special dreams? Imagine how Hugo feels when he frightens his friend Ferdinand. How about at the end of the story when he is with his friends again?

Picture clues – animal sizes

Look carefully at the scale of the animals in the pictures. Look at the size of Hugo and think about how big a lion would be. It wouldn't even fit on the page! No wonder the snail, the spider, and the tortoise think Hugo's dream is funny!

Enjoy the story – and the dreams too!

Wendy Cooling

Wendy Cooling

Reading Consultant

For Cameron who is already a lion.
With much love, ML

For Viv, many thanks, AB

Dorling Kindersley

LONDON, NEW YORK, SYDNEY, DELHI, PARIS,
MUNICH and JOHANNESBURG

First published in Great Britain in 2000
by Dorling Kindersley Limited,
9 Henrietta Street, London WC2E 8PS

2 4 6 8 10 9 7 5 3 1

Text copyright © 2000 Michael Lawrence
Illustrations copyright © 2000 Alison Bartlett
The author's and illustrator's moral rights have been asserted.

A CIP catalogue record for this book is available from the British Library.
ISBN 0-7513-7233-1
Colour reproduction by Dot Gradations, UK
Printed in Hong Kong by Wing King Tong

Acknowledgements:
Series Reading Consultant: Wendy Cooling   Series Activities Advisor: Lianna Hodson
Photographer: Steve Gorton   Models: Vanity Garrikk, Joe Eytle, Cherise Stephenson, Sam and Danielle Bromley

The Caterpillar That Roared

Michael Lawrence

Illustrated by

Alison Bartlett

A Dorling Kindersley Book

Now some caterpillars want to be moths when they grow up, and some want to be butterflies. But Hugo, he wanted to be a lion.

Every morning when he woke up he would gaze at himself in the mirror to see if he looked like a lion.

He would pull himself up as tall as he could, toss his imaginary mane... twitch his imaginary whiskers...

...and swish his imaginary tail.

But it was no good. He still looked exactly like a caterpillar.

So he would practise his **roar**.
At first the growl sounded
more like a squeak.

But as he practised and practised,
it began to sound like a very small,
very squeaky
little growl.

growl

Hugo decided to show off
his growl to his neighbours.

Nearby sat Winona the snail.
Hugo growled at her.
"What a funny noise for a caterpillar to make,"
Winona said.

"I'm not a caterpillar," Hugo told her.
"I'm a lion."
Winona smiled. "No, no," she said. "Not you.
I'd be frightened of you if you were a lion."

Next he met Ollie the Spider, lazing in the sun. Hugo growled. Ollie frowned. "Are you feeling alright, Hugo? I've never heard a caterpillar make a noise like that." "I'm not a caterpillar," Hugo said, "I'm a lion."

Ollie shook with laughter.
"That's the funniest thing I've heard all day.
You're no lion, my lad. I'd be frightened of
you if you were a lion."

Hugo went on his way, practising his tiny growl, and met Ruby the Tortoise returning from the shops. It had taken her three days to get there and back and she was very tired.

Hugo *growled* at her.

" I'm a lion,"

he said proudly.

"Oh are you, now?" Ruby said.
"Well, all I can say is it's just as well you're not.
I'd be frightened of you if you were a lion."

Hugo gazed up at the grass and
flowers growing high above him.
"If I were a lion," he said, "I'd be

taller and **bigger**

than the whole wide world."

He tried to stretch himself up and puff himself out but it didn't work.

Even when he shut his eyes he didn't feel any bigger.

He sat down on the riverbank and
looked at himself in the clear water.
He hoped to see a great big lion there,
but all he saw was a little caterpillar.

"*It's not fair!*" he wailed.
"Lions can be lions, so why can't I be one?"

Below the surface, Ferdinand the fish was preparing his dinner. Suddenly he saw something moving up above.

Through the ripples Ferdinand saw . . .

a huge and fearsome creature
        twitching its great whiskers,
            tossing its great mane,
                and swishing its great tail.

And then he heard . . .

...growl.

A great and terrible growl.

"It's a lion!" cried Ferdinand in fright, and he swam away as fast as he could.

Hugo was horrified.

"Come back, Ferdinand!" he shouted.
"It's me, Hugo. I'm not really a lion!"
But it was too late. Ferdinand was gone.

Hugo went home thinking about what had happened at the river. "If I were a lion," he said to himself, "everyone would run away from me. They wouldn't even stop to say hello."

And that night, as he snuggled down to sleep, he thought, "I'm *glad* I'm a caterpillar."

Activities to Enjoy

I f you've enjoyed this story, you
might like to try some of these
simple, fun activities with your child.

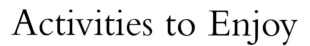

Ooooo Oooo

Animal make-believe

Flutter   Flutter

Roar!

Ask your child what
animal she would like
to be and why. Imagine you're
one, too. Then both pretend to be
those animals. Flutter your wings
like a butterfly, roar like a lion or
make a noise like a monkey. What
does your animal eat? Where does
it live? If you like, keep the game
going by pretending to be a
different animal.

Caterpillar puppet

Cut out several circles from coloured paper.
Overlap the circles slightly and tape them
together, or use paper fasteners so the caterpillar
can move. Tape straws, wooden skewers, or
lollipop sticks on either end to use as handles.
Finally, paint or draw a face on one of the ends.

Butterfly pictures

What will Hugo look like when he turns into a butterfly? Cut out a simple shape of a butterfly from a large sheet of paper. Fold the butterfly in half to make a crease and ask your child to paint one side of the butterfly. When she is finished painting, your child can fold the paper along the crease so the paint transfers to the other half. Then open the paper to see a beautiful butterfly!

Nature hunt

Why not look for caterpillars and butterflies in your garden or in the park? Or take a trip to the library to find out more.

Other Share-a-Story titles to collect:

This book
belongs to

....

Fun Ideas for the Storyteller

The Caterpillar That Roared is an engaging story about wanting to be different. Hugo the caterpillar longs to be a lion, but soon he finds out that being himself is not so bad after all.

Read on to find out how to get the most fun out of this story.

Snazzy word sounds

Enjoy the way the words sound! Look out for passages where you can join in with Hugo as he practises growling like a lion. Make the most of exciting lines such as *"Ferdinand saw a HUGE and fearsome creature twitching its great whiskers, tossing its great mane, swishing its great tail."* Reading with a touch of drama can really help children to get fully involved in the story.

Listen, look and share

Let your child take charge and turn the pages. Encourage her to join in with repeated sentences such as *"I'd be frightened of you if you were a lion."* Point to the words as you read them together. Your child will want to do more as she gets to know the story.